Traveling on Credit

Traveling on Credit

DANIEL HALPERN

The Viking Press / *New York*

ACKNOWLEDGMENTS

Some of these poems have appeared in the following magazines:

Antaeus: "Arriving," "Dutch April," "The Hunt,"
  "Latin Poem";
Choice: "Central Park," "St. John's Dream";
Esquire: "Afternoon Rite," "Scorpion Hunting";
The Humanist: "He Loves He Hates";
Mademoiselle: "Letter Home" (originally entitled
  "Note for Mother's Day");
The Malahat Review: "Pink Sharon," "Riddle II," "Riddle III,"
  "Riddle IV," "Riddle V";
The Mediterranean Review: "Frog Nights," "Fast Winters Ago,"
  "Sheldon's Poem II," "The Hitchhiker," "In Front of the Pornographer's
  Window";
New Directions Annual 24: "The Importance of Ritual," "Two Laments,"
  "Women," "First Date";
The New Yorker: "The Ethnic Life";
Partisan Review: "Spring Zoo," "Riddle I";
Perspective: "Women";
Saturday Review: "Traveling on Credit";
Shenandoah: "The Spanish School";
Southern Poetry Review: "Like Anyone";
Vertumnus: "St. John's Dream."

Contents

IV / RIDDLES

I / TRAVELING ON CREDIT

The Ethnic Life

I've been after the exotic
For years: champac
And patchouli in air, distant
Root scents, their smoke
Dazing rooms where dark men
Sit on legs
On rugs.

I ride teak trains
Through the Khyber Pass
Into Pakistan, and speak
Tongues I can't write.

My wife is young,
She turns to me from the East
After prayer—
Her black hair, her
Eurasian face spreading
Below the long eyes
Like Asian night itself.

On summer evenings before the monsoon
I meet my contortionist
Lover from India
Over Campari.
In her room my eyes roll
To paradise, click

Like a pair of Moroccan dice;
The undoing of her spine
Releases me from mine.

In my life
There is no room
For bikinis or Chanel,
Or the waxed beauty of the West. . . .

For years I've lived simply,
Without luxury—
With the soundness of the backward
Where the senses can be heard.

Over Campari During Mouloud

The streets fill up with brocade:
   Haik and week-day djellaba
Left hanging on a hook.

In the *socco*
   Men from Palestine,
Astute as Allah,
   Sell rock incense strong enough
To free all Morocco of djinns.

The stalls fill up with clay drums,
   Which punctuate the ululations
Of women wild behind the eyes,
   Heavy with Berber jewelry
And modena veils to hide
   The excitement of their mouths.

Beggars settle into familiar corners
   To reap the good feeling,
Eyeing the buses pacing in the crowd
   With passengers like memories
Encased in steel skulls.

Tangier, 1969

The Grasshopper

for Mohammed Mrabet

Mokhtar sat in his favorite café on the Rue de la Plage and smoked his *kif*. As the old countrywomen passed with their vegetables he lighted pipe after pipe. When the last of his tea was finally gone, he got up and walked down to the Avenue d'Espagne, where he came upon a grasshopper eating an onion. He got down on his hands and knees to have a closer look and noticed that tears were coming from the grasshopper's eyes. The onion got smaller and smaller as the tiny mandibles worked around it like spider legs. Mokhtar stared, and the grasshopper kept eating and weeping until the onion was gone.

Scorpion Hunting

The hills stretch under a green beard
And sleep. The mimosas
Purl in the soft wind that shakes
The palmetto, where scorpions
Creep in oval caves. Tucked in
Like switchblades their great stingers
Rest. In high boots we go
From mound to mound looking for holes.
I lick a long reed,
Feed it deep into an opening,
And when it moves
Farther into the hole, pull it
Back through the cave.
Then the scorpion is out,
Snapping his tail up as if it were cocked,
Pivoting in the dirt, watching
With a dozen eyes, breathing through its stomach.
A scissors cuts the poised stinger above the flesh.

The tail strikes, harmless as a wing
At the hand that lowers the bottle. . . .
We take it home to the women.

The Gossip

I'm a green bird.
DAVID WAGONER

This is no green bird, but gray with bright red
Tail and white chest. Polylingual, our gray

Can mimic the sound of every object:
At night, after the lights are put out, we hear

Silverware clinking on plates, the faucets
Going on and off. It's almost too much

When I hear myself on the telephone,
Or the doorbell ring. He has our life down

In his throat. Listening there in the dark
We fear what he could pick up next—the sounds

He might hear when he has gone through the noise
Of the evening. We know he's sitting there,

Waiting for something special to repeat
When he reaches for us in our sleep.

Spring Zoo

The children are too kind this year:
They've come to feed the mammals.
On the other side of glass
Snakes stretch their single extremity;
The baboons this season are as large as apes.

I watch the charges of *au pair* girls
Race the railing
For the elephants. On my bench
Down near the pond that's piled with seals
I share the fever, a jungle
Inmate of my own fantasy. The girls
Turn from sex to birds, or a hippo
Too vague to reproduce.

This year the children are just too kind:
They smile back at snakes or shake
An elephant's trunk.
The animals that are moving
Are unmoved by the round faces smiling
On the other side of steel. I feel Africa
Shiver in the trees, the children
And their attendants, the coupling
In cages. Having paid admission
I sit where the seals slide on moss

And let the big cats do my pacing.

Sailing to Africa

Where the railing turned back upon itself
I found her smoking
And stuffed two loud bills between her breasts

When I threw my hands on her
She let her eyes sink
And her hands drop to her skirt

We sailed toward Africa
Like a hinge loose in the wind

Island

Measured off the coast like a comma
The island, stroked by sea,
Settles, rearranges under the sun.

Men in boats filled with dazed fish
Ease onto the beach
Where women, dressed black as nuns,
Bid high voiced
Until their baskets flail with fins.

The sound of squid on stone
Consumes the morning.

The quick-eyed marketplace,
Barking with women,
Grumbles into noon:
    The barter and bid of wives
    While flies settle on the open meat.

Men with quick fingers in the grapes
Touch fields into ecstasy.

On the clearest days
Samos rises off the sea,
Like the steam of pots
Rolling fish edible.

Latin Poem

Peleus, shut up! Your foul-mouthed Thetis has dragged her
    wet tail
Over half the streets of Rome in search of Septimius
And our women laugh out loud in the marketplace at her
    lack of grace.
She is called "Muse of the midnight bed" by the loud boys
In the quarter near the Baths of Caracalla.

We befriended in the south of Apulia, and with good wine
In our hands talked of the sweet sluts we had laid
In the back streets of Rome, and of the years when we wooed
Young and old down the entire length of the Etrurian coast,
Where we trained by day for the high guard.

Peleus, remember how we stood on the beach of Phasis and
    laughed
At the breast-bare girls pulling in the nets of their fathers?
Friend! Where is the cock that placed three virgins in good
    standing
In a single night? That girl of yours plays with street boys
When your eyes are sleeping in the wine she pours for your
    dinner.

Good friend! Peleus! *Prius quam omnia mitiora*, think of
    yourself.
She has even today been knocking at my own door, the same
    door

You have so often passed through with my hand on your
    shoulder
When you came for talk and advice. She was here, friend,
Asking for my time and my bed. Peleus! Forget that slut!

The Spanish School

At five, on top of the refectory,
A boy steps up from the stair well,
Points a rifle to the tilting sun,
And puts a shot into the silence.

Pigeons and swallows start up
From the roof and rise in a vast wing,
Filling the air with sound.
Then the boy sweeps the roof

And spreads a layer of crumbs there.
In twos and threes the birds float back.
We watch the sun melt like a yolk
On mountains, behind walls of the school.

Dutch April

Tulips charge the grazing dikes, and I walk
In wood along canals, the water
Creeping from street to street where old men talk
Herring days. The breath of every flower
Hangs a scent on the air like laundry,
Each color boxed with its pedigree
Nailed against the wind. These colors recur
Like familiar faces on wine evenings.

A tulip Sunday: dresses are wings
Beating beyond my reach. In the sweet wake
The fish women swoon in their reverse make-
Up, hawking sardines fresh from the North Sea.

A lighter, poled from still water, springs
Its load of ripe Edam upon the quay.

The Party

It was a pale, tobacco light,
    or so it seems,
With women sagging under rings
And soft Negroes carrying
    silver trays,
The steam blending with the smoke
    of pipes and burning wood.

O the night was elegant, bright,
Lasting into the blue hours—
The sun, veiled by whiskey
    when it rose,
Caught ladies folded into gentlemen,
Gentlemen slipping their fine,
    pale hands at last moment
Back into gloves of Italian leather.

The Return

Dry leaves hang in wind. On the walls
Rakes throw from wire fingers a light
Back to the ball rolling in the trees.

Our men return in the autumn night,
Smelling of grass and the animals
They prod with sticks under the black trees.

At our gates the men load the air with calls
To wives and dogs; children come running
To bounce the chests of their fathers,

Smells of dinner seeping from the halls
Of wood houses. Weather is cunning
At night—it turns boys into fathers.

Buckskin Winter

We lived three months on pemmican,
Tracking back through a rough winter
To the caves where we shared beds
With ponderous bears shouldering
In and out of sleep. We set traps
Where the brown stick-brush jumped from snow
And caught rabbits dazed with cold,
Careless with hunger. The winter
Marched through five hard months and movement
In the snow had stopped before green
Faces started from the bleach. I
Wrote long letters home and began
Cleaning pelts stolen from winter.
The sun grew and all the bears stretched.

Waiting for Sunset

The panicles of witch grass splash
Their thin brushes out
Then freeze in air
Along the pond's edge.
I watch a wood ibis wade, stick-legs
Cutting the water in lines, its beak
Pressing below the surface
For fish
Or pond greens. This moment
Has stuck the red ball of sun
Between the legs of the ibis,
Colored the brushes of witch grass,
Hunched where water turns to land. . . .

I am waiting for the proper moment.

Arriving

On a day long and wet we fall upon
The city like tramps belched from all-night bus
Depots. Time is porcelain on the wall
As we step into the light. I will call
To the taxi stalling for his crude pay
Outside a bar, and if he comes for us
We will doze through falling streets, moving on
Until the heights break down before the bay.

At Steele's Motel a man behind a sign
Yawns his questions at us in hot clouds
And hands us a key, pointing where the night
Spills a crowd of different throats near a pine.
The cabin is a bed and desk—a shroud
Of moth wings on the screen, starving for light.

Sheldon's Poem I

for Aleister Crowley

Sheldon put on his female garb
And called himself the Lesbian Dandy.
He needed to laugh at the limits,
Push back boundaries and move where the air
Was asexual. He left New York
And his city life for the grass-
Lands of the West. He had North Beach friends
Where Broadway rubbed against Chinatown.
The twist was already the craze
In the expensive clubs. Sheldon spent time
Off Market, cruising sailors from Asia
On leave with an erection and some dollars
To soften it. The girls were fucking
Beatniks and Haight hadn't started up yet.

Sheldon's Poem II

The café sags out beneath a meager
Façade. Sheldon feeds us lines from New York
And the crowd slides by. I must say I prefer
This table where the wine sits without a cork.
Sheldon says, "A lot of chicks in velvet
Dresses won't talk to you if you look like
A creep," and goes on to the ethics
Of fountain pens. His eyes swim as the wine ticks
In his head. The sun nods on a hill like
A hand, and we move on to *espresso*.

My friend flaps in the small wind—she is high
And the day's words dance in her calico
Hair. Her smile squats in the street near a fly
As Sheldon starts himself up again, spill-
Ing his life as the sun enters the hill.

Spanish on the Block

My neighbors speak Spanish, grumble trash
Into pails at dinnertime. On the street
A Negro with white shoes comes at nine
And plays blues from Nashville. Women

Walk the street braless,
Their men pile cans of beer on the curb
Till the sun goes down, then, on faster things,
Throw coins near a wall and roll dice.

The men toss coins to a wall, the women,
The slim women who walk weird beats
With tropical skirts scaling their thighs,
Smudge the air with Puerto Rican oils.

I cross the wakes of scent they leave
And consider their loud price,
Drink beer in their bars and sit next to them
Feeling like a neighbor.

At night I dream of knives, the clinking,
Blink at the flash from bright steel
And turn from sleep when their victims moan,
Waking into an explosion of sun

And Spanish neighbors talking below.

Central Park

There was a Negro with white shoes who played
That Sunday. The cops wore macaws
On their shoulders and all the children
Held balloons gassed so they shot for height.

The people were happy, played silver
Flutes that closed on other sounds like handshakes
Dancing in trees, and the trees
Danced, holding their dancers tight.

The Negro tapped his foot
Till the shade inched from his bench.
Steel bands rocked the air, birds
Hung upside down from the sun.

Traveling on Credit

They would think up trips on Sundays—
Traveling to Lahore via Persia,
Sliding through the Khyber Pass,
Dropping into India like Polo.

The trips began off Fire Island
On a beach day with high red winds,
Swimming nude in South Bay
Together. The residents looked away,

Cared for their gardens which suffered
From the whip of the salt wind
And the Patchogians, who
Came with bayberry sandwiches

To hawk their bodies in the sun
And hurry back on the last
Watch Hill ferry. They lived
In Bayberry and thought up trips

With the marina's population
(A Calcutta of boats)
Looking on from polished wood.
They were, for the most part, in love,

Traveling, Sundays, to Lahore
In three cars with two wolfhounds,
Four afghans and a setter—
A Packard, a Daimler and a Ford.

They were set on Lahore:
Stops in Izmir and Isfahan,
The long crawl through Persia.
On Sundays, in fine weather,

They set out with a pocketful
Of visas and rolled east, content
With itineraries of sand
And postcards back on the weekend.

II / FROG NIGHTS

First Date

By number
I find her house haunching
On a minor street:
A tired circus of old wood
With windows caught
In a perpetual blink,
A trapezoid of memory
Tucked in by grass
That rolls in remembering
Decades
Of watering and clipping

Two-storied,
The upper leans on the lower
Like a squared elbow.

She comes,
A footfall of sound,
Opening the door
Onto the intricate nature
Her living has sewn
Into the broken silence.

Making It in Kansas

I name you
Chiropodist Mother,
Corn-cutter from Kansas
With consistent arthritis.
Your daughter
Has puffed up her small breasts
In a secession from parentage,
Succeeding in the expansion.

I seduce you with manners
Vibrating from a pragmatic upbringing;
Your consent of character
Brightens the vigor of your offspring—
Allows the pleasure of my hand.

Unconfined
I am at ease at tea in the afternoon,
Verbal and poised,
Enjoying the subtle acknowledgment
Shared in the applause of two ladies. . . .

Flesh grows strange attachments.

The Pick-up

In new tanker jackets we hitched
Up Van Nuys Boulevard
With cheap girls in mind.

Westerns at the Fox attracted them—
High hair, short skirts,
They smoked like women and eyed the door
For boys to make it with
Later.
With hair Brilliantine-straight,
White peggars, shiny shirts rolled at the cuffs
And bright socks,
We knew that.

The trick was to pick out the prick teasers,
Then eye the ones who really put out.
They were quieter, concerned
With finding the best of us
To unzip and move on
In the back seat of a car parked on a back street.

I don't think any of us
Saw a movie straight through—
The boys moved in pairs from row to row
And the girls stayed in pockets,
Discussing the movement around them,
Eating popcorn.

We found two up front with heavy perfume
And big tits;
We offered them some Coke
And they declined,
Thinking of Spanish Fly
And gearshift knobs in locked cars.
We moved in on each side
Slipped an arm around them and watched
The film
Until our hands fell to their female flesh.
We waited for the slap or scream
And when it didn't come
We squeezed
Further,
Pushing into their salty mouths
Our Doublemint tongues.

When the lights came on we slipped our sweating hands
Out of the elastic on their chests
And moved them out into the blue L.A. night
To the garage that once served as clubhouse.

They never said two words, serious
And well-built they came right along
With our hands on their shoulders
And theirs around ours. . . .

We turned on
Special red dims
And guided our girls
To separate bunks:
Upper and lower.
They climbed in without a word or laugh;
Mine sighed like a pro I knew of

As I pulled her onto the mattress
And stumbled up the buttons of her blouse.

When I had her the way I wanted her
I slipped
Off my own clothes
And with two hot hands

Hung my new tanker on the hook with her bra.

Pink Sharon

for Push

Pink Sharon
Is the lipstick in her purse.
I look to her feet
And in my head fasten my hand
To her ankle.

They said, "If you can't
Put your hand round a girl's ankle
Don't marry her," and I've been spanning
Ankles for years.

She sits next to me on the train
And rattles her purse—
I see the Pink Sharon,
The small ankles,
And drop a coin. I bend for it,
My hand falling to her ankle,
My fingers finding each other,

And I look into her eyes
And she looks into mine,

And I say, yes
And between my fingers
She says, yes.

Hitchhiker

A momentary altering of her thumb
Pulls me to the curb.
She climbs in and begins to wonder
About my hat and gaudy Vivaldi
Spinning off the radio:
She thinks I might rape her
And when I make no movement like that
She says,
   Don't you ever try anything?
And I say,
   No, too shy.
   Do you like this kind of music?
   Yeh, she says,
And begins to hum,
A bar off,
But sweetly, like a pretty girl,
Well poised,
As if I weren't there.

After a while
Her words get whiny
So I tell her I'm turning.
At the light she gets out
Saying thanks with a nod,
And moves to the other side of the street,
To hitch back where she came from. . . .

Afternoon Rite

Across the way
In another tragedy
A cat and a man
Share a doorway
Each the other's
Indifference
As I yours
As I undo
Trickery
Above your hem
Undo the support
Of your decoration
In a snap

The silk of your skin
Exposes its minor run
Which
I fear
I have made too much of a fuss over
Again

She Wears Her Breasts Blinded

Her slim breasts stiffen out of sleep,
Out-staring the pause
Caught in the morning sky:
Silent prayers for a smooth hand.

I watch with eyes freed from discretion
As she dresses, uneasy in the light,
The last of her drowning
In the machinery of the dress.

I cannot comprehend female weight

They ride like blond fists
Shoved into soft gloves,
Blunted and anchored
And free
From the pressure of my eyes.

He Loves He Hates

for Carolyn

He loves her he hates her
He leans her in dream
On a linnet's thin thread
Of flight
Casting in red air,
The afternoon leaking
Through the trees, over
The hill, loose
Down the circle
That appears again behind him.

He loves he hates
He leaves her staring
At bird flight, loves
Her back from the dark,
Hates the gradual drift
Her thoughts take
In sleep,
Loves the gentle turning, her
Body slipping out of sleep.

Fast Winters Ago

Fast winters ago I stilted
On three-by-threes past your window:
Ten, in love, and half my height now.
Looking back nothing has wilted
In that chamber where I locked you,
Fast winters ago, to let your hair
Drop low enough for me to pursue
My captive to the hidden room.
The old vines push in for a look
And see you counting in a chair,
Waiting for the sound that will loom
In the air like a wave and hook
Itself in your brown hair to climb
Hand over hand back up through time.

Balaparté

For an hour your hand has moved your face
Into a false brightness. From a red tube
Your mouth jumps to life. A black stick traces
In your blank eyes, and a silver jar lubes
The face that went dry parties ago.

The mirror confuses you by the slow-
Ness of its resiliency. Stroke by stroke
You become the girl of our first party,
Cornered by a man you finally broke
With to spend weekends at Balaparté
With me. Now I snap where you can't reach
In a roomful of the perfume you cling
To. Painted and bright the other girl sings
Again, as if we were on that first beach.

Frog Nights

The frogs outside my window hog the night—
Their sound is of a certain art
That has wandered beyond the tight
Beat from a polyrhythmic heart.

I turn you over and move
From a favorite direction,
Sending you to that teeming pond
Where nothing is left undone.

And there is no need to disprove
These various ways we grow fond,
In a night, of things that respond.

The black is pregnant with croaking
And different loves just beyond
This room, where in disguise we move.

Women

She dreams
Smooth green snakes
On rainy nights

It seems
He read her
Rough copies of great poems

She would fake
Understanding so he
Could go to bed happy

She thought it right
Things went on this way
For he brought home

Beautiful things from the city

Pastimes

"Why, you're a genius," she said.

A natural enough comment I thought
As I glued the last side to my plane
And started papering the fuselage.

I could see her on the couch,
Her hands clicking with needles and wool.

"Why, you're a genius," I said.

She nodded,
Thinking the remark natural enough
As she placed the last stitch in a sleeve.

It's not bad living with a genius
We both think
As we glue and stitch through life.

Two Laments

The walls of her house are dark
Where rain has turned to wine.
The Cherokee neighbor grumbles cactus
Into the ground and salutes her.

Tamed by static
The laundry clings to her like children.

He only springs for sadness

Is her thought as she roams the house
Gathering errands in her arms.

In the citrus light,
Her hair tied tight in a snood,
She puts a sponge to water
And shines the cedar of her house with lemon
Wax.

The antique clock sleeps in iron, drumming
A progression of fingers to her head
Where the number for her love
Waits. . . .

For sadness

She sighs,
But it shines the stainless,
Wanders in and out of rooms beneath her hair
And paces in her eyes.

When the bell rings,
And she goes running for the phone,

    There is only sadness for tone.

II

The rain the garden is not gentle;
Rather, it is rough with bark
Gathered from the high tree:
Sweet maple, leaves
Like his open hand.

Like moss
His tracks are tacked
To the ground
Where they gather
Surface.

On the pock-marked patio
The water pools itself
And sways;
The rain burns the lawn
And the hydrangeas revive.

    He only springs for sadness,

And spring moves in from the cold
With light rain
Dripping from burgundy shingles.

A dropping of feet into mud.

III / THE IMPORTANCE OF RITUAL

The Initiation

Akela

That night the palominos went crazy
After the lightning struck one
Asleep on its feet in the corral.
They reared, ran for fences that pushed them back.

The men came in from the rain and took us
Out barefoot into the moonless night;
The light hit down the valley,
Climbed back up the mountain and dropped
Like a wave.

Shaking in the bang and rain of the night
We marched like women into the trees,
Pushed on by robed and booted men.

The ceremonies I had heard of—I felt the blades
Come down with the light,
The trees exact from us their favors
As we tumbled through their generations,
Pushed up the unending trail by men with slow smiles.

Below, far in the valley where we lived, the horses
Pawed the dirt raw, swayed to the boom
Bruising the night with a dark flat sound.

Then we were alone. Light cracked in the trees.
The oldest among us took us down,
Took us where the rain fell half as hard,
And climbed alone till he saw light
Steady on the hillside, hurled bright against the black.

The sound of dogs took over
When the horses shut their brays into yellow barns
Thrown open by the storm.
Moment to moment the dogs grew louder, closer.

Then we all climbed trees, the bark breaking down the white,
Soft surface of our sleeping feet.
We held on like leaves till the light came leaping
Before the dogs, and the trees quit their movement.

We climbed down, full of the wet night,
And trailed the path
Back where the palominos swatted flies with their tails,
And shuffled in their leather.

We climbed down through the high-hung country like men,
Stiff, proud,
Full initiates of that far valley.

The Importance of Ritual

for N.

"This pillow's nothing," she thinks
All night. "To get your head
Off the bed you have to fold it
In threes."

   And the black drops her.

In the morning
She throws the urine
Out the window and applies
Florida Water to her cramps,
Which fade—
Waves to ripples.

   Garbage trucks grind up
   The silence around her coffee.

She opens the door
And the postman falls through the porch.
"I could stamp straight through it
Too," she thinks.

   "The violence, the violence
   Is terrible," she thinks.

Someone told her:
"Put sweet basil behind your ear
And quick, turn on it,"
Catching the pocket of scent
Hanging like hair.

She placed the herb on her ear
And turned to it, catching it,
Losing it,
The wind
Eating it.

The pillow,
The cramps,
The coffee next door,
The postman descending.

   Florida Water and basil.

In a heavy chair, time for her
Is the growth of nails
Through her clenched fist.

Like Anyone

for Sarah

She had theories: like every eel
Going to the Sargasso Sea before dying.
Like salmon. Like Moslems.

Like doing minuets to calm down,
Or birds hating tilting houses.

Her house tilted and the birds stayed away—
Nut hatch, grosbeak, cardinal. . . .

She saw pigs as horses
When they were stranded, straddled
In the snow to their bellies,
And believed in white witches—
Males who predicted like crazy
While they danced and looked
Like anyone.

Like not washing her hair
To keep it full.
Like the wooden fish
She sucked for health.

Theories were her slaves,
And she was young with hair
White as witches.

The eels in her smokehouse
Hung from their chins near the bowl
Where wooden fish soaked in oil.

While her hair thinned the birds flew
By the tilt of her house,
Like her life at the slight angle
She lived it.

Following It Down

Think how you will follow it down
The road where a wheel spins empty
And the blue weeds turn on themselves
As the sun beats time against the sky.

Think how you will follow it down
To the banks of a jealous river
Which races winter only
And turns its back to the heat of summer.

And when it settles like a fly
On the hand of a clock ticking
Seconds, breathing into time,
Keep an eye free for the beast that flashes
Out of the cobalt balance.

The Clepsydra

Water drums the thief.
  Water clocks eat
  Weeds in the heat
Of a day already brief.

On the stream boys flow
  By like eels
  Beyond the feel
Of hands that reach below

The line where breathing stops.
  Thief! cries the water.
  Clocks and otters!
Where? Where? scream the cops.

The Hunt

Setters mark the turf and run
For quail, spring to a point where wings
Fold and flying stops. Water on branches,
In beads—the sun explodes, sparks
The eyes of the setters, of the quail.
The hunters sweat on steel, taut jerkins
Stiff, and eye the bush for game—
Their dogs have eyed it to the ground.
Slowly they move in, stealthy and clever,
Guns in air. The scene tightens.
The quail feel the stare of the setters,
Of the hunters—the smell of their metal
And jerkins—of life in the morning
When light is still low. The men drop
To their knees in a familiar pose,
Eyeing the V, lining up life
In their blind sights. A finger squeezes
Action into the cold morning,
And the quail jump from sound
Into air.

In Front of the
Pornographer's Window

Two-dimensional and touched
Up
The ladies pull us
From our pace.
We pause with interest less than casual
And begin to imagine,
Leaping into rooms we keep out of sight.
The flat flesh jumps
Out
And becomes personable.

Format to format
Our eyes bounce narrow with indifference
Over the rude flesh,
Waiting for a likeness to pull away from a cover.
Then we stall
A moment,
A silent group of flattered men
Scanning pink headlines
Until one of us moves,
And we're all away—
A flock
Scattered by a stone.

Perverts

I

A lonely little man.
He lives with a white cat
In a house too big
Since his wife left.

II

I never thought much
About the creeps in the park,
The ones who come out with the night
To lurk in red socks behind the gladiolas
Planted by the city.
All they do is watch couples
Steal sex off the benches.
I've even seen them hang from trees
And gape at the tight skin
Of a young girl's face!

III

Some girls leap
From his eyes like waves,
While others dive
Fathoms below his belt—

The place where insects
Move in his hand.

He almost lets them go as they jump,
But they return
Once out
To roll through the fingers
He keeps out of sight.

IV

Oh, he's patient all right,
Sitting on his bench,
Crossing one leg over the other,
The bones clicking under his chino trousers.

Girls walk by
With mothers for eyes.

He can wait.

It's What's Worthwhile

It makes life interesting—
Men on the floor,
Sick, drunk,
Crazy.

But what does it mean?
What's in it to stall
And have a look
With urine hung in the halls
Like webbing?
What's in it for me to stand
And have a look?

It's what's on the floor
That makes life worth walking into—
The position you're not caught in
That attracts the crowd.

There's always time for a look
Before we continue on,
It makes the rest worthwhile. Yes,
There's forever that moment
When we put time in our mouths like caramels
And let it melt to the floor with our eyes
And for the first time taste salt.

Speed

Shunted through the measured interiors
Of needles spitting slogans into blood,
The collage climbs inside the elbow, floods
The flow of arteries bathing that slow
Encasement which moves its exterior
Like something roaming blindly the old haunts
Of fantasy. Unevenly the mind
Of that soaring beast pales, slowly goes blind.
What fiction of the wandering eye taunts
The high weather blowing behind a face?
Alien textures from a misspelled place?
This world is a seduction of the sense,
Cloth on top of flesh that seems to vanish
Between the fancy pickets on a fence.

The Inverted Crucifixion

for Maurice

Because he thought the emulation bold
And the times were ripe for humility,
Peter felt it right when the Romans told
Him, upside down was the final decree.

Pinned like a poster to wood, feet in air,
His head dangled where once his sandaled foot
Stood, and sweeping round the base, his hair—
Fire in dirt. To the cross he was put.

When Christ lifted from rock out of mourning,
Peter remained, hanging like a comic,
The complement of right-side up: a warning
Against the powers of rhetoric.

Later, after two nights turned to morning,
Peter slid from the nails, a Catholic.

St. John's Dream

After the trumpeter placed his last note
Upon the air, Jerusalem in shambles,
The nocturnal woman stood with the moon
At her feet and a dozen stars
Circling in her hair, while another
Pulse raced in her womb. A divine man-child
Rocked in the fluid, waiting for his wave
To break upon the new shore. In the dark
Of his mother grew the masculine light,
But hanging at her waist like a dream
A red dragon waited with seven heads,
Patient for the moment when the offspring
Of that heavenly couple, fruit
From the highest house, would fall within reach.

Pittsburgh / 1952

My aunt is taken to her room
With a plate of whitefish
And left

Our family is used to age

My cousins sit on the porch
And tease the dog
While I try and think
Of a sister at school
In Arizona

My uncles
Throw the war back and forth
At the table
Mother serves the meal

After dinner we go outside
And sit in the Tierneys' garage
Then on the Klausens' fence
To eat raspberries

At ten the mothers appear
And one by one
We disappear

In our house
My aunt is asleep in the chair
With her mouth open
The relatives have collected their things
And are shaking hands
Goodnight

Acrostic Poem

After 9:00 climbed its way up the
Long clock, our time snapped into place.
Lanky, you balanced a delicate word
And played invisible ping-pong at
Night on the C.O. roof like a Nepal friend.

Dining rooms and romance: an eye ripe as
Indian curry, pushed into
New shades of red sometimes by a stray word.
You are a low chanting in the corner.

Raging returns me to you
In an idle moment. An evening with
Two of you, two of me, and wine—
Calling for the lasting roommate,
Howling for the one that would make us four.

Letter Home

You savored my conception
In the dark:
A new forest of quick water.

From you
I dropped
Into the breathing world,

Clenched in needing,
Undoing the house
With simple screams.

You held me, a reluctant puppet,
Teaching my loose legs pride.
The pride learned leaving.

This year the fast ends,
The misdemeanors of childhood
Turn silly in my open hand
    and I
Having learned the tight lyrics of growing
Can show you
That the long gift comes back.

IV / RIDDLES

I

Your digs will neither rouse nor rib
Me; of your kind there isn't one
I couldn't put on,
Feel the whole thing was a cinch. Remember,
I've been saddled with more:
My very nature once carried existence—
I swung my blond hair
And felt the wind keep pace upon my chest.
Now I merely tamp impatience
Into unripe moons of dirt.
I may be foolish,
Lose my head now and then in a wind
Or chomp at the bit heading home,
But nothing more—there are
Pleasures to consider: a wardrobe
That's admired and can excite
The deviant among you, or girls
Who dream of me, hot
To trot the landscapes of their dreams.
No, things are not bad—
I may very well be the only stud
Among many more dashing
To walk this earth upon his own good luck.

II

With a body full of vertebrae,
Dark muscle,
The insect moves on a long
Slow curve, too fast for us to focus
On, too quick to stop in flight
For a moment
And register impression.

We hear the sound it starts
Up from, and see the room
It makes for itself alighting
Only. Its home is a shell
That's shed when life
Is over. —That
First and final trip alone
Is its funeral.

III

It is my pulse
That is father
To all others,
My hands,
Sure and deft,
That shape men's lives.

I speak every tongue
Known to man,
And yet they learn
My language as children,
Learn that my demands
Are unending,
My rule, final.

My beat has kept me alive
Forever,
I've had a part in every history
Though you will find
No trace of me
Anywhere.

But I am everywhere
And nowhere——

And I have the final word.

IV

Your arms cover half
Of everything
We know, allow
The quiet pulse of our time
Together. It is
In your presence that owls hoot into blackness
While others sleep. We move within your dark
Skein—you allow us to face
The face of our ambitions,
Give us our secret smiles
That later become public.

I would venture to guess
That it was in your presence,
And perhaps because of it,
That we began in this world, which is half yours.

V

I lurk in shadows,
Venture out, thin-legged,
In the dark.

It is true,
I am older than anything
I hide in,
My ancestors are found in stone.

Women hate me,
Wish
To be rid of me,
Though I would not think
Of touching them.

For hunger only
I stay here,
Hard, fast,
My name, in part,
Keeps their world alive.